The Minute Hand

is the 1986 Lamont Poetry Selection

of The Academy of American Poets.

From 1954 through 1974 the Lamont Poetry Selection supported the publication and distribution of twenty first books of poetry. Since 1975 this distinguished award has been given for an American poet's second book.

Judges for 1986: Philip Booth, Louise Gluck, and Mary Oliver

The Minute Hand

Jane Shore

The University of Massachusetts Press
Amherst, 1987

Library of Congress Cataloging-in-Publication Data
Shore, Jane, 1947–
    The minute hand.
    I. Title.
PS3569.H5795M5   1987   811'.54   86–24983
ISBN 0–87023–570–2 (alk. paper)
ISBN 0–87023–571–0 (pbk. : alk. paper)

British Library Cataloguing-in-Publication Data are available *for Howard*

Even while we speak, the hour passes.
Ovid

ACKNOWLEDGMENTS

The following poems (sometimes in slightly different form) appeared in these magazines:

The Antioch Review: "A Clock"; "Eighth Notes"; "A Luna Moth"; "Wood"
The Iowa Review: "High Holy Days"
The New Republic: "Pharaoh"; "Dresses"; "The Glass Slipper"; "German Weather House"; "Solomon's Sword"; "Persian Miniature"; "Shuttle"; "Friday Night Fights"
Pequod (in *Secret Destinations: Writers on Travel*): "The Island"
Ploughshares: "Aubade"; "Anthony"; "The Russian Doll"; "The Other Woman"; "Two figures"
Poetry: "Young Woman on the Flying Trapeze"; "Tender Acre"
The Seattle Review: "Thumbelina"
The Tufts Review: "The Ark"
The Yale Review: "The Game of Jack Straws"

I would like to thank the National Endowment for the Arts and the New York Creative Artists Public Service Program (CAPS) for their support. And my gratitude, also, to Mekeel McBride, Lorrie Goldensohn, Gail Mazur, Frank Bergon, and Philip Levine, whose patient criticism helped shape these poems.

CONTENTS

The Minute Hand

A CLOCK

Summer twilight tamps down the farmhouse roof.
Kneeling in his lettuce patch, the farmer
stares through the wrought-iron bars of the III—
a rusting harp that heaven plunked down
beside him, junk too heavy to haul away.
He squints at his wife beyond the IX
tending her even rows of greens.
Rising and falling between them,
the steady hands of the Planter's Clock
skim the white enamel dial that time has turned to cream.

The sun dips and disappears
as the moon rises over the minute hand.
The pageant glides by, on gears.
Up in thinner air where the moon aspires,
a cornucopia spills stars and ripening planets—
a tomato Mars, a turnip Saturn, and four
greenbean comets whipping their tails.
Gigantic as the silo, an ear of corn
floats light-years over the barn.

Rooted in the ticking rim of earth,
the farmer and his wife can never touch.
Brighter than the moon, an onion sheds its light
on their awestruck faces morning, noon, and night.
If only she could slip inside
her pretty trapezoid of home
and cook her husband a good square meal,
but the farmhouse door is painted shut

3

and the curtains drawn—
hiding the feather bed, the empty crib,
the cupboard filled with loaves of bread.

High in that harvested astronomy,
the onion is incapable of tears.
Whatever Intelligence placed it
like a highlight shining in the farm wife's eye,
also chiseled the lists into the bedrock
of the planting charts on which she stands—
tables of days and months and seasons,
killing frosts, auspicious times to sow—
indelible as the stone tablets of the Law.

The farm wife casts her vision higher even
than the moving parts of heaven.
Do other worlds like hers exist
in rooms in distant galaxies—
exact copies of her farm
with weather vane, weathered barn
and a husband bent upon his knees,
praying or weeding,
his face, a wrinkled thumbprint?

Like opening a familiar book,
the illustration always stays the same
no matter what time of day she looks.
The same furrows stitch the fields;
and haystacks, heaps of golden needles,
dot the farthest pastures, the last of which
drops neatly into the horizon's ditch.
Dig potatoes now. Thin the beets.

It's five to nine. Years later than she thinks.
She feels the earthquake each minute makes
behind that shaking scenery,
heartbeats coming from so far away
she has to cup her ears to hear them.

PHARAOH

So as not to be lonely
in the afterlife
the boy-king was buried
with his most cherished things

items he would need
on his journey
toys, enough food
for a lifetime, maybe more

a golden cage
on whose perch
his canary
still sings like a rusty hinge

his throne
his cup
a spoon or two
made of solid gold

urns filled with oil
urns filled with honey
some broken dishes
plenty of wine

his gold mask
a perfect likeness
on which his highness
crayoned a faint mustache

his silk tunic
a supply of papyrus
an ivory comb
with no missing teeth

a mirror on which
to breathe a cloud—
the tomb's only weather
that, and dust

his dog
a golden ball
two old servants
curled at his feet

under the bandages
pharaoh, a boy,
buried with his hands
in his pockets

a star chart
carved on the ceiling
under which
a deep healing is taking place

YOUNG WOMAN ON THE FLYING TRAPEZE

Shooting with his Bolex,
my father kept nature in perspective.
He caught the trapeze artist catching
his partner in midair, swinging

in and out of my line of sight.
I was five. In nightmares, the body
falls straight into the dreamer's eye
who wakes before hitting bottom.

Did I blink then, did I glance away,
the moment that she tumbled
like an angel out of heaven?
I don't remember, but I saw her fall.

My father slows the projector down
frame by frame; the trapeze artist
aims for her partner, and somersaults.
Her partner's wavering hand

connects with her sequined wrist;
but his other hand misses, clamping
shut on the air that frames her,
no connection, her body blurring

its slurred speech, as scanning
the sawdust floor, the camera locates
the broken italic of her flesh.
No connection! I can't remember

no matter how many times I see her,
no matter how many times
my father runs the film.
Projecting in reverse, he has her

climb the ladder of light
one more time, for my benefit;
but he can't rescue her
from gravity forever.

Backward, she bullets up toward
the bull's-eye of her partner's fist,
her face enlarged in its unknowing—
as she lands back on the platform,

squarely on her own two feet!
Spliced into the same reel, unreal
documents of the commonplace.
A picnic underway. Then it is Sunday.

The living room upholstery is brand new.
The Frigidaire is white-enamel white.
Then, a lucky break to catch this,
I am crawling, hoisting myself up

my mother's skirts to take my first
steps, fighting to keep my balance,
staggering toward whatever it was
I reached for out of the camera frame—

held and lost in that drifting
instant of attention,
from which the body performs
its miraculous escape.

THE RUSSIAN DOLL

Six inches tall, the Russian doll
stands like a wooden bowling pin.
The red babushka on her painted head
melts into her shawl and scarlet
peasant dress, and spreading over that,
the creamy lacquer of her apron.
A hairline crack fractures the equator
of her copious belly,
that when twisted and pulled apart,
reveals a second doll inside,
exactly like her, but smaller,
with a blue babushka and matching dress,
and the identical crack circling her middle.

Did Fabergé fashion a doll like her
for a czar's daughter? Hers would be
more elaborate, of course, and not a toy—
emerald eyes, twenty-four carat hair,
and with filigreed petticoats
like a chanterelle's gills blown inside out.
An almost invisible fault line
would undermine her waist,
and a platinum button that springs her body open.

Now I have two dolls: mother and daughter.
Inside the daughter, a third doll is waiting.
She has the same face,

the same figure,
the same fault she can't seem to correct.
Inside her solitary shell
where her duplicate selves are breathing,
she can't be sure
whose heart is beating, whose ears
are hearing her own heart beat.

Each doll breaks into
a northern and a southern hemisphere.
I line them up in descending order,
careful to match each womb
with the proper head—a clean split,
for once, between the body and the mind.
A fourth head rises over the rim
of the third doll's waist,
an egg cup in which her descendants grow
in concentric circles.

Until last, at last, the two littlest dolls,
too wobbly to stand upright,
are cradled in her cavity as if waiting to be born.
Like two dried beans, they rattle inside her,
twin faces painted in cruder detail,
bearing the family resemblance
and the same unmistakable design.

The line of succession stops here.
I can pluck them from her belly like a surgeon,
thus making the choice between fullness
and emptiness; the way our planet, itself,
is rooted in repetitions, formal reductions,

the whole and its fractions.
Generations of women emptying themselves
like one-celled animals; each reproducing,
apparently, without a mate.

I thought the first, the largest, doll
contained nothing but herself,
but I was wrong.
I assumed that she was young
because I could not read her face.
Is she the oldest in this matriarchy—
holding within her hollow each daughter's
daughter? Or, the youngest—
carrying the embryo of the old woman
she will become? Is she an onion
all the way through? Maybe,
like memory shedding its skin,
she remembers all the way back to when

her body broke open for the first time,
to the child of twelve who fits inside her still;
who has yet to discover that self,
always hidden, who grows and shrinks,
who multiplies and divides.

EIGHTH NOTES

For George Shore

In the twilight of their stores,
the butcher scatters sawdust,
the baker ices a name on a cake,
the owner of the dress shop
lowers the radio as his daughter
practices arpeggios and scales.
A sale is on. Business is slow.
A floor above his head,
she lurches through ten seconds
of "The Minute Waltz,"

glancing at his fakebook,
A Thousand Standard Tunes.
If only she'd accompanied him
on "Georgia on My Mind"
and "Star Dust"; tagging along
on his years of one-night stands
on the road with Clyde McCoy
and his famous Sugar Blues Band.
In black-and-white glossies,
he's Clark Gable as a skinny Jew,

a boy in a man's tuxedo.
In the wash of memory, the gray
evening jacket turns light blue,
the shirt white and the bow tie red;
he's crouching on one knee
as though proposing to the camera,
blowing his sax's golden note
through the pre–World War II
unruffled palm trees, before marriage
cut short his tour of duty.

Marooned on the piano stool
on the stage of her grammar school,
she plunged into the medley
she knew by heart—the first few bars
of "Georgia . . ." And forgot.
Then stuttered them out again.
And like an amnesiac, woke
to the auditorium's tense silence,
then applause—each a slap
in the face for the absent music.

Everyone makes mistakes, he said.
He tallies up the day's receipts.
It's 1959. His New York buddies
washed up on the Jersey Shore.
The Goldwyn Girls, Follies of '35.
Any one of those showgirls
might have been her mother—
even Theo, of the flawless smile
and filthy mouth, platinum hair
whipped into peaks and swirls,

ran off with a drummer
and lost her voice. Her autograph
dips and glides across the heart-
shaped bodice of her strapless.
Near the empty dressing room,
her father works a crossword puzzle.
On their racks, the dresses sway—
the collar's faint necklace of scent,
metal teeth locking along the spine,
cloth—like air—whose careless hand

can touch a body all at once
and everywhere. She turns the page.
Her thumb returns to middle C.
The metronome's hurrying the girl.
The little soul trapped inside
whose weight swings hip to hip
keeps issuing its sharp commands.
If it hadn't been for you
he could be leading his own band. . . .

On late Sunday afternoons
they stand together in the window
undressing the mannequins
—the redhead and the blonde—
pursed lips, radiant stares, heads
bald under all that gleaming hair.
On tiptoe, she dusts their faces,
stroking the feathers
across the azure eyes
that never blink or tear.

As if asking for a dance,
her father steps up to the blonde,
her rigid arms embracing air.
With quick twists,
he unscrews her slender hands—
a scar circling each wrist—
and gives them to the girl,
careful not to chip the cool,
red ovals of the nails.
And then the arms come off.

He shimmies the satin dress
up and over the hips and head.
I'll be right back, he says,
and goes into the racks
to choose the next week's dress.
In the dark mirror of the window
the girl freezes in her pose
before the other pair; wearing
the mannequin's stiff blonde wig
like a helmet over her own dark hair.

ANTHONY

Your absent name at roll call was more present
than you ever were, forever
on parole in the back of the class.
The first morning you were gone,
we practiced penmanship to keep our minds
off you. My fist
uncoiled chains of connecting circles,
oscilloscopic hills,
my carved-up desk, as rippled as a washboard.

A train cut you in half in the Jersey marshes.
You played there after school.
I thought of you and felt afraid.
One awkward *a* multiplied into a fence
running across the page.
I copied out two rows of *b*'s.
The caboose of the last *d* ran smack against
the margin. Nobody even liked you!
My *e*'s and *f*'s traveled over the snowy landscape
on parallel tracks—the blue guidelines
that kept our letters even.

The magician sawed his wife in half.
Then passed his hand through the gulf of air
where her waist should be.
Divided into two boxes, she turned and smiled
and all her ten toes flexed.
I skipped a line.
I dotted the disconnected body of each *i*.

At the bottom of the page,
I wrote your name. Erased it.
Wrote it, and erased again.

THUMBELINA

Thumbelina, poor sleeping child,
swaying in the hammock of a leaf,
nested in my left hand the whole
summer of my seventh year,
her skull just the size of my thumbnail,
her bird heart ticking against my pulse.
Only a child, I was an only child
small for my age, but a giant
towering over a clump of crabgrass.
A belly button in the dirt,
the anthill was the slave plantation
I oversaw, ants laboring
in the fork-raked furrows,
hoisting heavy sacks of cotton—
crumbs fifty times their body weight.
To be a giant, you must learn to step
softly, carefully, so as not to hurt
the working earth.
That year in school I was learning
how to add. The backyard thundered
with my mother's yelling. "Ssh.
Don't wake the sleeping Thumbelina,"
I'd whisper into my left hand.
"Don't hurt the sleeping child,"
the shell of my left hand echoed.
At home I was learning to tell time.
Each night when I tried to sleep,
I heard the alarm clock's jeweled

movement, seventeen diamond planets
on saw-tooth wheels orbiting a ruby sun.
But something else was ticking
in another part of the Milky Way.
A cloud-spasm in the utter darkness,
something else was swimming into the galaxy.
Who could imagine anything so foolish
as a child the size of a thumb,
a replica, a shrunken opposite,
a speck of sand that no amount
of wishing could dislodge.
Inside my mother's body, a girl-child
already as big as a lima bean
was growing. But the child I carried
with me, who slept the sleep
of a speechless animal,
I carried for my own protection.
I never raised a hand against my mother
because the hand can crush what it protects.

HIGH HOLY DAYS

It was hot. A size too large,
my wool winter suit scratched.
Indian summer flaring up through fall.
The shul's broken window
bled sunlight on the congregation; the Red Sea
of the scarlet carpet parted the women from the men.
Mother next to daughter, father next to son
flipped through prayerbooks in unison
trying to keep the place. Across the aisle,
my father wore a borrowed prayershawl.
A black yarmulke covered his bald spot.

The rabbi unlocked the ark
and slid the curtain open. Propped inside,
two scrolls of the Torah dressed like matching dolls,
each, a king and a queen. Ribbons hung down
from their alabaster satin jackets;
each one wore two silver crowns.
I wondered, could the ancient kings
have been so small? So small,
and still have vanquished our enemies?

The cantor's voice rose
like smoke over a sacrificial altar,
and lambs, we rose to echo the refrain.
Each time we sat down
my mother rearranged her skirt.
Each time we stood up
my head hurt from the heat, dizzy

from tripping over the alphabet's
black spikes and lyres,
stick-figure batallions marching to defend
the Second Temple of Jerusalem.

Rocking on their heels, boats
anchored in the harbor of devotion,
the temple elders davenned Kaddish, mourning the dead.
Our neighbor who owned the laundry down the street
covered his left wrist out of habit—
numbers indelible as those
he inked on my father's shirt collars.
Once, I saw that whole arm disappear
into a tub of soapy shirts,
rainbowed, buoyant as the pastel clouds
in *The Illustrated Children's Bible,*
where God's enormous hand reached down
and stopped a heathen army in its tracks.
But on the white-hot desert of the page
I was reading, it was noon,
the marching letters swam, the regiments
wavered in the heat,
a red rain falling on their ranks.
I watched it fall one drop at a time.
I felt faint. And breathed out sharply,
my nose spattering blood across the page.

I watched it fall, and thought,
you are a Chosen One,
the child to lead your tribe.
I looked around the swaying room.
Why would God choose me

to lead this congregation of mostly strangers,
defend them against the broken windows,
the spray-painted writing on the walls?

Overhead, the red bulb of the everlasting light
was burning. As if God held me in His fist,
I stumbled down the synagogue stairs
just in time to hear
a cyclone of breath twist through
the shofar, a battle cry so powerful
it blasted city walls to rubble.
And I reeled home through the dazed traffic
of the business day—
past shoppers, past my school,
in session as usual,
spat like Jonah from the whale
back into the Jew-hating world.

THE GAME OF JACK STRAWS

One at a time from the pile
each player in turn tries

to remove the Jack Straws—
the miniature hoes, shovels,

ladders, pickaxes, rakes—
without moving any of the others.

Light as a bird bone,
the fragile sword fallen free

from your lucky scatter
is easily yours.

You may keep it and attempt
another. Using the tiny hook

or your fingers, you barely
touch a wrench when the hammer

below it stirs.
On your next turn, careful

as a paleontologist,
bones craning over bones,

you lift a pitchfork
cantilevered on a scythe

balanced on the flat blade
of an oar which rests

against the nervous edge
of the saw—one body

touching the body of another
which has touched another's

body, and so on, that graveyard
of relations better left buried

and forgotten like the casual love
you fall out of and out of.

The more chances you are given,
the more the diminishing returns.

If you had the hammer
you could fix the stairs

that lead to the basement
that shelters the rat

that shows you his nest
where the nails are hidden.

Though your heap of Jack Straws
keeps growing, the player

with the most points wins.
Why is an arrow

worth less than a saw,
and a saw worth more than a hammer?

It's a foolish carpenter
who doesn't know the value

of his tools.
The pile dwindles to two.

You'll play until love
either kills or heals you—

like the young husband
who, at daybreak, extracts himself

from his sleeping bride;
careful not to wake her,

lifting his trembling body
pale and weightless as straw.

GERMAN WEATHER HOUSE

Spinning high above the weathered barn,
the axis–mundi of our muddy yard,
the copper weathercock
rules with an iron will,
a will identical to the arrow he perches on.
On one squeaky leg, he swivels south,
southeast. The wind can't flutter
his battered tail. He swivels north.
Gaining in velocity,
the wind follows him obediently.

Or so he thinks. Directly overhead,
the dime–sized sun has just begun to spread
a dime's worth of warmth.
Smiling Brunhilde pops out her door
and stands on the porch at full attention.
A guardian of good weather,
her right cheek bruised blue
where the paintbrush missed her eye.
Her braids, two blonde antlers,
stick straight out of her head.
Fuming behind his matchstick door,
her grumpy husband, Hans,
picks up where she stopped dusting
the black ladder of thermometer
and rinses out the mop.

Marriage isn't made in heaven.
Like Heraclitus, neither

can step onto the same porch twice
during the same weather.
The wheel their feet are glued to
binds them together for better or for worse,
her cheerful face opposing his at every turn.
But when his cloudy eyebrows begin to gather,
Hans throws a trenchcoat over his mossy lederhosen
and lurches forward like a second hand
while Brunhilde lurches backward
toward the midnight of her door.
Above her trembling lintel,
herds of thunderclouds stampede the roof,
slamming Brunhilde's door shut, locking her

inside the dark particulars of home.
Mopping the floor, she wonders
if she's responsible for the storm.
The armor guarding Brunhilde's heart
is a cotton pinafore.
Cowering behind her flimsy door,
she softly calls her husband home,
but Hans feels most at home
outside, conducting the Wagnerian sublime;
his anger, the leitmotif that sparks repeatedly
like a trick candle that won't blow out.

But high above the weather house,
the weathercock thinks that *he*'s the maestro!
Dead center in the hurricane's eye,
he's just ordered the sun to rise
for the second time today!
Dawn's alarm clock, aren't all moving bodies

subject to his whims?
Why else would those two below
pop out their doors like manic cuckoos
and jerk along their miserable circle
unless he were their oracle . . .

And the eye of the storm blinks, and moves on.

FRIDAY NIGHT FIGHTS

Slamming down the phone,
she breaks the connection from coast to coast
and shifts to his side of the bed.
What would he do, if he were here now?
The TV screen blooms in monochrome
with the sound off:
two boxers stagger to opposite corners
of the ring to recuperate from Round 4,
where the challenger spat some blood out
and got his second wind.

The champion, a black boxer in white trunks,
sizes up the challenger,
his negative wearing black; and dances him
to the ropes with systematic punches:
a right, a left uppercut, his gloves
attracted to the bruised magnet of that face
interchangeable with his.

She's absorbing this,
how neither boxer will give in;
even when the challenger's fist recoils
and a rose explodes in the champion's brain,
and he falls across the column
of his partner's body, embracing it,
sliding his arms down the torso
until his face is level
with the black elastic waistband, and beneath,
the cup that guards the man's genitals from harm.

No breastplate shields the heart
from injury. No armor. The ringing begins
and she holds her breath for the count—
seven, eight, nine—her hand wavers
over the receiver. And far away
he hears those words still ringing in his ear,
and can't call them back.

TENDER ACRE

As you slept, your pulse
flickering on your neck like a trick of light,
I thought how, earlier, beside the sleeping shape
Adam labored the whole night to stay awake,
afraid she'd vanish in the morning with the moon.
Out of the earth sprang the planet's
blurred, unpredictable life.
The pulse of the near hill,
or was it the shudder he was born with,
rocked him. The animals, also,
that yesterday brushed like wind against his body,
were now given form. On a branch,
an icicle began to melt.
It hung, glistening and patient,
while a zipper of vertebrae inched all the way down
its back. Then bands of bargello
stitched the skin—tiny saw-tooth flames
of dull gold and rust, rust and gold.
This he named *snake*.
On the topmost branch of the tree,
a bird bristled with little white thorns.
Then each thorn fanned out like a palm-frond
and the bird flew away.
All day, Adam watched and listened,
but he couldn't name his loneliness—
the long "oh" of sorrow, the "ooh" of hallelujah.
Eleven curved knifeblades
of his rib cage, and the twelfth

that cut his flesh without injury,
he accepted,
as he accepts these other gifts placed before him.

All night, he memorized her human shape,
so that later, were she not there,
his memory could reconstruct that absent body
from the air, and wrench him from his solitude
before the tender acre cradled her.

TWO FIGURES

negotiate their way across a frozen lake,
careful not to touch, careful not to upset
each other's balance. The house is quiet;
I have been thinking about them all evening
and now, my window spills across the ice
the narrow path of light they are walking on.
It's hard to see but I think the smaller one
is a woman, her parka sparks some color—
though most colors go neutral in the dark.
When I breathe out, I breathe a lake
on the inside of the glass.
For a few seconds, it totally obscures them,
until the little lake I've made starts melting
and the two come clear again.

I can't hear them but I imagine the man
is remembering another lake, how his skate blades
cut through the black shine beneath him,
his body shattering the lake's pane of glass.
I think the woman wishes she had been the one
to cast her scarf across the ice and rescue him,
but now his presence only makes her lonelier.
I think he's just said something that's hurt her
enough to make her stop.
He must be sorry, because he's stopped too.
I can't see them but I feel the cold
between them, and must wait until the lake
on the window clears again.

Now one of them is talking instead of listening.
One of them is in danger. Their words fly
like white birds out of their mouths.
I wish I could stop them a minute; stop them
from hurting each other, but which words
would I put back in their mouths?
They are almost on the bank below me
and soon they will want to come in.
If only I could hold them off a little longer,
for a little longer keep them anonymous
and safe, before they will become me.

WOOD

At eight o'clock we woke to the chain saw.
The clumps of pine
quivered as the empty flatbed lumbered by,
printing snake skins up the snowy road.
The telephone company was thinning out the woods.

That afternoon, we snowshoed to a neighbor's farm.
They were gone, but their brown cow leisurely chewed.
She tried to ignore us, keeping an unforgiving eye
on us, and on the rags of grass beneath the snow.
—The sound her teeth made tearing
was like a seamstress ripping out a seam.
The enormous head swayed and dipped—
it scared us too. A skein of spittle
dangled from her lower jaw;
her tongue was big as a boot, awkward and dull pink;
her black leather nostrils snorted
a storm of cumuli, hot and white.

It got colder. Dusk held the trees in amber
—the ones, that is, left standing.
Around the fresh-cut stumps, sawdust, a fringe of twigs
were mashed into the snow.
The telephone company had cut down a tree
to erect, in its place, a sort of monument to a tree—
an imported, pitch-stuck pole with its own tin badge and number
linking house to house and voice to voice.
Later, when we fed the fire, the embers
glowed under the logs which the flames systematically ate,

nibbling slowly, deliberately,
from left to right. Like reading.
Sometimes, a fire devours a book all at once
in one sitting; or slowly, disinterestedly, leafs through it,
turning its pages to ash one by one.

There's pleasure in watching it ignite
and flare, pleasure that does not want to stop
—in looking around the room
and throwing in anything that will burn.
A paper napkin thrills the flame,
but briefly; a chair causes greater excitement—
its rush seat, a catherine wheel sputtering, shooting off sparks.
—And punching a hole in plaster
to snap off the laths ribbing the walls;
and peeling shingles from the gray
bird wings of the roof
until the whole house burns with pleasure.
But then the fire died down. We closed the book.
A few of the ashes' soft feathers
drifted lazily up the chimney shaft
into the vanished daylight.

THE ARK

On the avenue below, they file past—
Two and two, two and two,

And are recorded. Men and women
Climb the ramp and enter my body

To be welcomed; as Eve welcomed
Adam, who bore her, and broke him

Uninjured by her departure.
And the children, each with his small grief,

And the animals, each with his complaint,
Issue from the planet that would keep

Its strict count. Male and female
He made them, beasts unlinked by gender;

Monstrous or innocent, they fill me,
Who will carry them to safety.

And the dove now circling the tree,
Once circled this wilderness inside me:

An instrument meant to receive life
And not to judge it.

PERSIAN MINIATURE

Two hairs plucked from the chest of a baby squirrel—
the brush of the miniaturist freezes an entire population.
Within each quarter-inch,
a dozen flowers puncture the spongy ground,
and even the holes where tent poles stuck
bear ornamental weeds.
Upon a wooden balance beam—this painting's equator—
a cat is prancing.
Other animals are eating or being milked:
three spotted goats, a suede camel,
half a donkey's face lost in an embroidered feedbag.
Under a canopy, seven elders in pajamas radiate
like spokes around a bridegroom;
white beards frost the elders' chins.
Outside, a fat iron cauldron squats upon a fire
whose flames spike up golden minarets.
A kneeling boy pours coffee;
his pitcher handle, the size of a human eyelash,
is larger than the bridegroom's mustache.
A wedding! Is the bride asleep somewhere?
The bride's attendants hover in tiers
like angels in heaven's scaffolding,
but heaven, here, is the hanging gardens,
or maybe the tent poles hold the heavens up.
Lappets of a tent fold back
on a woman holding her soft triangular breast
to an infant's mouth. The rug she sits on
flaps straight up behind her, like wallpaper.

One-sixteenth of an inch away,
a ram is tethered to the picture frame,
but where's the bride going to fit?
In the left-hand corner of the painting,
across what little of the sky remains,
two geese fly in tandem, pulling two wheels,
two mechanical knotted clouds.
Maybe they are pulling a storm behind them.
Crouched, swirling above the human event,
if the storm fits, it could ruin everything—
smash up the whole abbreviated acre,
flush the bride from sleep—
while the bridegroom sweeps it all away
and enters her innocent tent like thunder,
shattering the distance he's had to keep.

THE GLASS SLIPPER

The little hand was on the eight.
It scoured Cinderella's face, radiant
since her apotheosis; blue dress,
blonde page-boy curled like icing on a cake.
The wristwatch came packed in a glass slipper
—really plastic, but it looked like glass—
like one of my mother's shoes, but smaller.
High transparent heel, clear shank and sole,
it looked just big enough to fit me.

I stuffed my left foot halfway in,
as far as it would go.
But when I limped across the bedroom rug,
the slipper cut its outline
into my swelling heel.
No matter which foot I tried,
I couldn't fit the ideal
that marks the wearer's virtue,
so I went about my business
of being good. If I was good enough,
in time the shoe might fit.
I cleaned my room, then polished
the forepaws of the Georgian chair;
while in the kitchen, squirming in her high chair,
a bald and wizened empress on her throne,
my baby sister howled one red vowel
over and over.

Beside the white mulch of the bedspread,
my parents' Baby Ben wind-up alarm
was three minutes off.
Each night, its moonface,
a luminous and mortuary green,
guided me between my parents' sleeping forms
where I slept
until the mechanism of my sister's hunger,
accurate as quartz,
woke my mother and me moments before
the alarm clock sprang my father to the sink
and out the door.

Seven forty-five. His orange Mercury
cut a wake of gravel in the driveway.
Like a Chinese bride I hobbled after him,
nursing my sore foot in a cotton sock.
Cinderella's oldest sister lopped off
her own big toe with a kichen knife
to make the slipper fit, and her middle sister
sliced her heel down to size.
Even the dumbstruck Prince failed to notice
while ferrying to the palace
each of his false fiancées,
the blood filling her glass slipper.
The shoehorn's silver tongue
consoled each one in turn,
"When *you* are Queen, you won't *need* to walk."

THE OTHER WOMAN

In the first dream she is the enemy,
spangled in love's armor, wearing
the sweater she knitted for him,
and she looks prettier than in the photo

you discover in his bottom drawer
that puts her in perspective—
all scowls and squinting at the sun,
unflattering, as he has captured her.

Possession is nine-tenths of the law.
The dream's percentages are never fair,
reminding you how comfortably she fits
within the familiar outline his body

shapes around her; her face partially
hidden by his, they are laughing at something
private, because your mind still must admit
to the old alliance. In time you dream her

exactly the way you want to see her,
ugly, and one night you catch them
making love in the back seat
of the car you are driving.

For once you think you are in control,
but you must keep one eye on the road
and not swerve from your original fidelity,
while in the rear-view mirror, they sink

below your line of vision. How did you
maneuver yourself into this position?
—as earlier, safe in your single bed,
your parents' night-cries woke you,

and, locking you out of intimacy,
they more deeply locked you in.
In the next dream, with teeth and nails,
tearing at her placid face, you awake

surprised at your capacity for violence,
how good it feels. And you shift
into a higher gear. You're driving
through a blizzard and she's beside you,

strapping herself in. Crazy, that your dream
should place a seat belt so conveniently,
and she, compliant as a test-car dummy.
Misery loves the company inside us

even when we'd be better off alone.
You make a U-turn and invite her home.
Climbing the stairs, the two of you
reenter the battlefield of your bedroom.

Compatriots now, on the double bed,
you ask what she intends to do, now
that she is almost ready to let him go,
but she's not herself, not the woman

in the photo, and by now you've forgotten
what brought you two together—
oh, here he is again, shouting up
through the floor for you both to pay

attention. He slams the porch door shut.
From your window, the red arc
of his sleeve is the last of him you see.
He revs the engine, and aiming the car

at the foundation of the house,
he ploughs into the snowbank below you.
Backs up and ploughs again.
And nothing you can do can make him stop.

CREATURE COMFORTS

At first, I thought that drift of fur was dust.
Closer, saw teeth smaller than strings of seed pearls,
the body curled stiff around the mouse-trap's spring—
as if mouse and trap had animated the other;
the mouse, triggered by hunger; the trap, by touch.

If love is more than a matter of territory or hunger
that drives us together against our will,
should I have escaped sooner, or adjusted to a life
in which one lover keeps torturing the other,
each too paralyzed to kill?

SHUTTLE

"Burning in this strange, this ill-fitting body
of my marriage, I settled too early with my wife,
crazy, frightened, two days out of college.
For fifteen years, I watched darkness construct
a kind of house around my life. When morning came,
I thought I'd never have the courage to shake
loose from her arms, the arms of my children.
This morning on the plane I had this thought:
for fifteen years marriage was my address
and I was its homesick tenant.
Now my life is opening like a dream
with all its familiar furniture, even
a flight of stairs, dizzying and continuous,
that I begin to climb.
I feel like the bird you brought home:
rocketed to your apartment in a cardboard box
with symmetrical punched-out holes
to let in a little light and air.
I watched you quaking, handle the quaking thing
clinging to the bars of its cage.
For hours I've watched it, pretending to read.
I can't keep my eyes from the animal—miserable,
hunched rigid on its perch, catatonic
from the absent flutter and touch
of other wings; refusing seed, refusing water,
in terror of your hand. The bird worries me,
now that I'm free, shocked by light again."

SOLOMON'S SWORD

Today, I walked down to the field
where they measure the wheat into sheaves,
and saw the boy bending over his sickle
harvesting with the others,
only the half of him showing,
his legs disappearing in the waist-high grain.
Twelve years since the night I was delivered of him,

and I lay back on my bed,
my body still hurting where he had torn it.
He was given to me. I was told what to do.
After I nursed him and they left,
he fell asleep on my bosom, his breath
sweet from the little I could give him.
Under his weight, I fell asleep
and dreamed my body was a huge stone wheel
turning against its adversaries,
laboring against the bodies
that worked so hard at pleasure
to rid themselves of pleasure.

When I woke, or dreamed that I woke,
I turned and found
his little body lay beneath me like a stone;
he made no cry at all.
I took my breast and nursed him,
his mouth filling up, his mouth
that demanded nothing, and the milk started

spilling across his cheeks,
into his nostrils, his open eyes,

and I thought, why should I not
share this abundance
with the infant sleeping in the next room,
his mother asleep beside him,
—we three were alone in the house then.
The blade that had earlier worked on me
still lay on the moonlit table—

I carried him to her, he weighed no more
than he had when I earlier held him,
he was no heavier than hers—

and I replaced her baby with the dead one.
In his wisdom, Solomon
should have slain the infant;
it would have been fair to cut it in half
and deliver me from my grief
a second time. It would have been fair
to divide the grief equally,
now that one has more and one has less.

DRESSES

On wire hangers, on iron shoulders,
the dresses float in limbo,

flat-chested spinsters who will
not dance. It is night,

the hands of the clock circle
their twelve black mountains,

upstairs the children are dreaming,
and over his red and black inks

the father figures the books,
the store as dark

as the inside of the safe.
Blouses like airy armor, trousers

that marched off the cutting table
through the needle's eye.

Dresses, it is your nature
to be possessed. With feverish hands,

your jailer will free you, undo
the two pearl buttons on your cuff

while her lover hitches up your skirt,
his rough wool against your silk . . .

eventually those caresses will wear
you away. One day you will be

the crushed body in the ragbag,
the purple in the pauper's closet,

the hand–me–down passed from one sister
to another in a distant state.

Your pockets will fill with her
perfume, ticket stubs, loose tobacco,

the telegram that changes everything
the moment it is read, and memory

makes you too painful to wear.
Houndstooth, black-watch plaid,

mauve, teal, hunter–green; shades
flaring and dying with the seasons—

except for the mannequins heaped
in the cellar under the store.

Rashes of plaster dust cover
the gash where the wrist screws

into the arm; modestly dusting,
like talcum, the chipped torsos,

the bald heads, bald crotches,
and around each beautiful eye

the corona of ten spiked lashes.
In the morning, the older daughter

descends the fourteen stairs
to the store and tries on

the frothy, white organza strapless,
dragging its hem like a tide

across the fitting-room floor;
and there you are in the mirror,

up to your old tricks.
She'll curtsy for her adoring father,

while her mother—
mouth bristling with straight pins—

kneels at her feet. The cash register
resumes its noisy music, browsers

breeze in and out of the swinging
door. Sooner or later, each of you

will attract your customer.
Not on your own volition will you

enter the blazing street and pass
the sister whose smooth back

you pressed against so long ago.
Not on your own volition

will you dance at a daughter's wedding,
dance unwearying until dawn

with energies not your own.
Nor for beauty's sake alone will you

be chosen from among all the others,
when, in severe folds, you will outwear

the body that entered your body willingly
once, and lost herself there.

A LUNA MOTH

For Elizabeth Bishop

For six days and nights
a luna moth, pale green,
pinned herself to the sliding screen—
a prize specimen in a lepidopterist's dream.

Tuesday's wind knocked her off the deck.
She tacked herself back up again.
During Wednesday's rain she disappeared
and reappeared on Thursday
to meditate and sun herself,
recharging her dreams from dawn to dusk,
and all night draining the current from
the deck's electric lantern.

A kimono just wider than my hand,
her two pairs of flattened wings were pale
gray-green panels of the sheerest crepe de Chine.
Embroidered on each sleeve, a drowsing eye
appeared to watch the pair of eyes
on the wings below quite wide awake.
But they're *all* fake.
Nature's trompe l'oeil gives the luna
eyes of a creature twice her size.

The head was covered with snow-white fur.
Once, I got so close
it rippled when I breathed on her.
She held herself so still,

she looked dead. I stroked
the hems of her long, sweeping tail;
her wings dosed my fingers with a green gold dust.
I touched her feathery antennae.
She twitched and calmly
reattached herself a quarter-inch west,
tuning into the valley miles away
a moment-by-moment weather report
broadcast by a compatriot,
catching the scent of a purely
sexual call; hearing sounds
I never hear, having
the more primitive ear.

Serene
in the middle of the screen,
she ruled the grid of her domain
oblivious to her collected kin—
the homely, brown varieties of moth
tranced-out and immobile,
or madly fanning their paper wings,
bashing their brains out on the bulb.
Surrounded by her dull-witted cousins,
she is, herself, a sort of bulb,
and Beauty is a kind of brilliance,
burning self-absorbed, giving little,
indifferent as a reflecting moon.

Clinging to the screen despite my comings
and goings, she never seemed to mind the ride.
At night, when I slid the glass door shut,
I liked to think I introduced her

to her perfect match
hatched from an illusion
—like something out of Grimm—
who, mirroring her dreamy stillness,
pining for a long-lost twin,
regarded her exactly as she regarded him.

This morning,
a weekend guest sunbathing on the deck,
sun-blind, thought the wind had blown
a five dollar bill against the screen.
He grabbed the luna, gasped,
and flung her to the ground.
She lay a long moment in the grass,
then fluttered slowly to the edge of the woods
where, sometimes at dawn,
deer nibble the wild raspberry bushes.

AUBADE

Each day, each morning, before the sun can touch
one edge of anything, within the oak's shadow
an unfamiliar bird begins to sing.
Against the sky,
the leaves the dark has polished are now
shingled like the grisaille wings of the bird,
and the whole garden's gone over with the same
meticulous hand, the grass held down
with long, even stitches, as morning settles
on the rosebush, anchored by each thorn.
On the near hill there are flowers like small fires.
Inside the house, a man and a woman are sleeping.
Daylight's an infusion of pain so slight
each barely feels it ribboning down the spine
until the bird begins to call them
back into the landscape their closed eyes
labor to admit.
For an instant, the man sees himself
twist up to light as he reaches for the woman
preparing to open herself to him,
as later, earth will take his body wholly in.

THE ISLAND

On one side, a series of marshes.
On the other, the ocean level as a skillet.
Across the bay, the wooden church
suffers under the weight of its weathered circumflex,
beneath which, every Sunday, the natives come to pray,
and every Tuesday, hold town meetings.
And once, when the movie people sent a scout,
—"You want to rent a room?"
—"No. I want to rent the island,"
they threw him out. He ferried back that very day.
The latticework on each widow's walk,
like the cable knitted into each fisherman's sweater,
is as individual as a thumbprint.
The summer bungalows look like pairs of scuffed brown oxfords
that hiked to sea from far inland
and stopped short at the harbor.

Mornings, tennis balls
criss-cross the Common like tropical birds.
Back and forth they fly, fat, chartreuse, echoing across this
aviary with the lid off.
And occasionally, the tracks of baby strollers
struggle up the clay cliffs, irregular as molars.
Some dunes are now off limits, like the Parthenon.
The commissioners would like to bulldoze
the whole community of nudists,
who, by noon, in most weathers,
expose their white triangles and stripes

and look like negatives of themselves.
Puckered beer cans stud the public beaches, and here and there,
an evicted hermit crab bleaches.

This morning, a Spanish freighter almost sideswiped
the island's cliffs. The sailors were friendly.
They waved tee shirts from the upper decks
as if hoisting up a patchwork rainbow,
and maneuvered through the channel, blowing kisses.
I watched the ship get smaller and smaller
(almost colliding with a rust-pocked trawler),
small enough to squeeze through the neck of a bottle,
and then, the horizon swallowed it.

I unfurled my towel, and read, and slept awhile
(the water was too cold to swim),
and wondered about the glass armada
bobbing along the coast's two hundred mile limit.
At high tide, a bottle detached itself,
and riding the assembly line of waves,
it tumbled up the beach faster, faster,
a lost collie to its master,
and landed six inches from my sunburned feet.
I held the bottle up to light—
a dozen highlights oiled the glass—
and saw a five-masted warship, uncollapsed,
with its antique mizzens still intact.

Crawling like an ant along the hull,
the ship's unlucky stowaway tried to shout
but the plug was stuck in the bottle's throat.
Upon the pages of the sails,

he scrawled his message in letters the bottle magnified
gigantic as a billboard painter's:
Each night, I dream that I walk the plank
of my wife's long hair, but I can't drown.
And now, I've sailed right into your own two hands.
I've survived my island of a shipwreck.
Someday, from your shipwreck of an island,
I will rescue you.